Angry Arthur

Hiawyn Oram Satoshi Kitamura

ANDERSEN PRESS

Once there was a boy called Arthur.
He wanted to stay up and watch
the western on T.V.

This Book Belongs to:

. . . .

For Tremayne and Piers

First published in Great Britain in 1982 by

Andersen Press Ltd., 20 Vauxhall Bridge Road, London SW1V 2SA.

This paperback edition first published in 2008 by Andersen Press Ltd.

Published in Australia by Random House Australia Pty.,

Level 3, 100 Pacific Highway, North Sydney, NSW 2060.

Colour separated in Switzerland by Photolitho AG, Zürich.

Printed and bound in Singapore.

10 9 8 7 6 5 4 3 2 1

British Library Cataloguing in Publication Data available.

ISBN 978 1 84270 774 6

"No," said his mother,
"it's too late. Go to bed."
"I'll get angry," said Arthur.
"Get angry,"
said his mother.

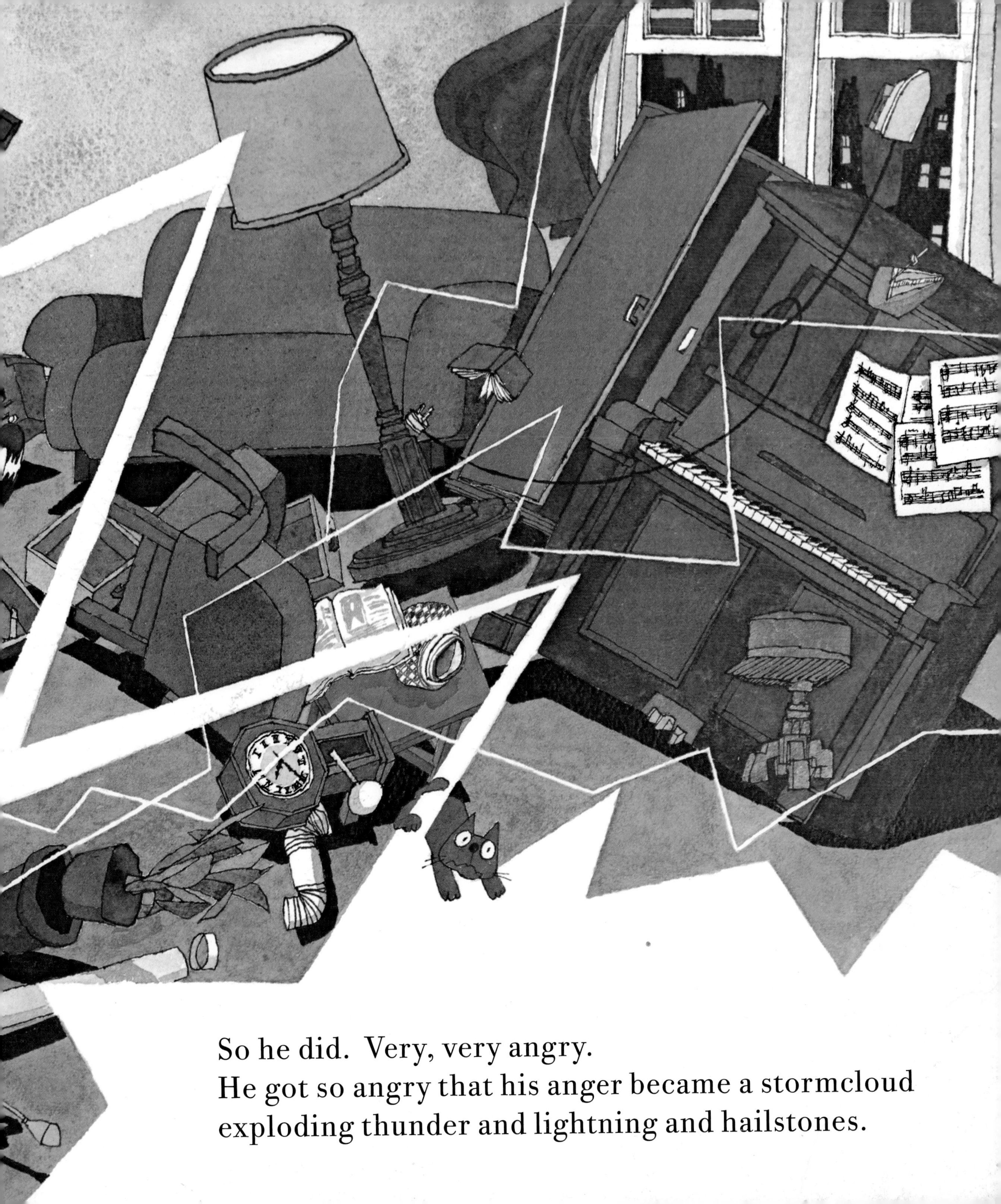

So he did. Very, very angry.
He got so angry that his anger became a stormcloud
exploding thunder and lightning and hailstones.

"That's enough,"
said his mother.
But it wasn't.

Arthur's anger became a hurricane hurling rooftops and chimneys and church spires.

“That’s enough,”
said his father.
But it wasn’t.

Arthur's anger became a typhoon
tipping whole towns
into the seas.

TYPhoon Tea
14
PUTNEY

“That’s enough,” said his grandfather.
But it wasn’t.

Arthur's anger became an earth tremor cracking the surface of the earth like a giant cracking eggs.
"That's enough," said his grandmother.
But it wasn't.

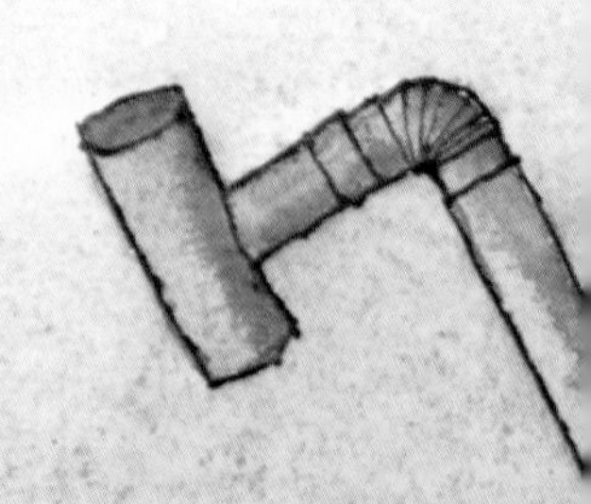

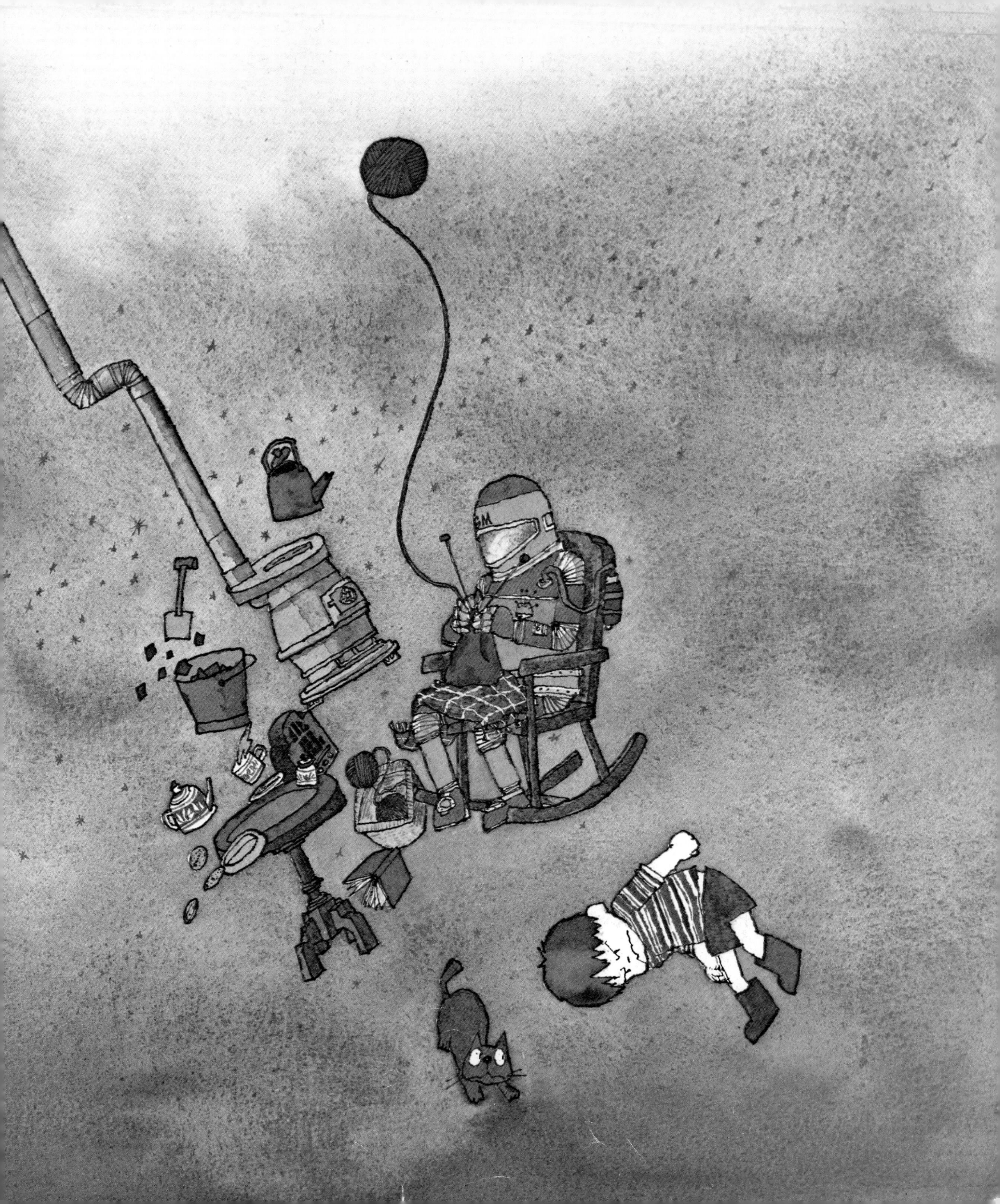

Arthur's anger became a universequake

and the earth and the moon

and the stars and the planets,

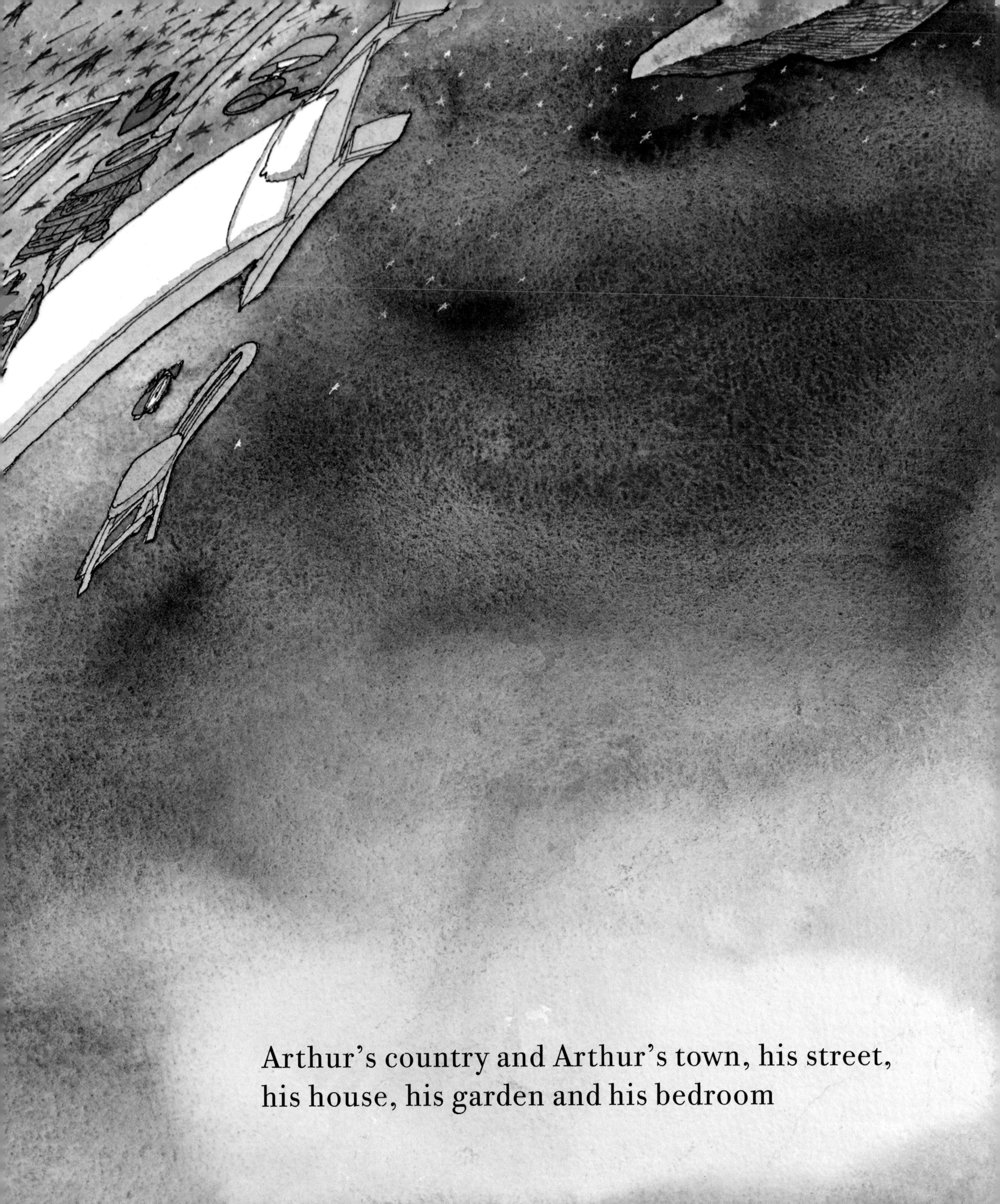

Arthur's country and Arthur's town, his street,
his house, his garden and his bedroom

were nothing more
than bits in space.

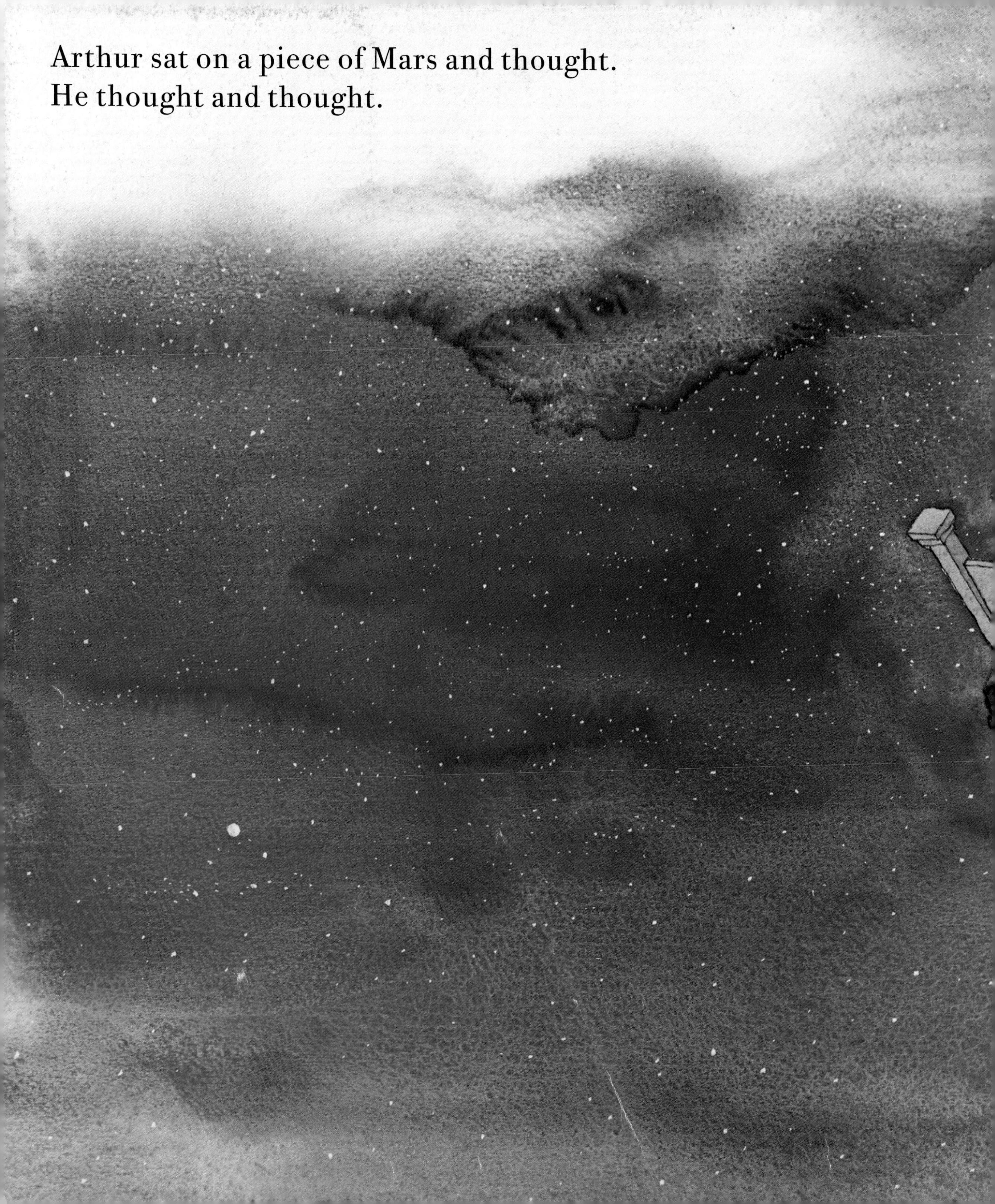

Arthur sat on a piece of Mars and thought.
He thought and thought.

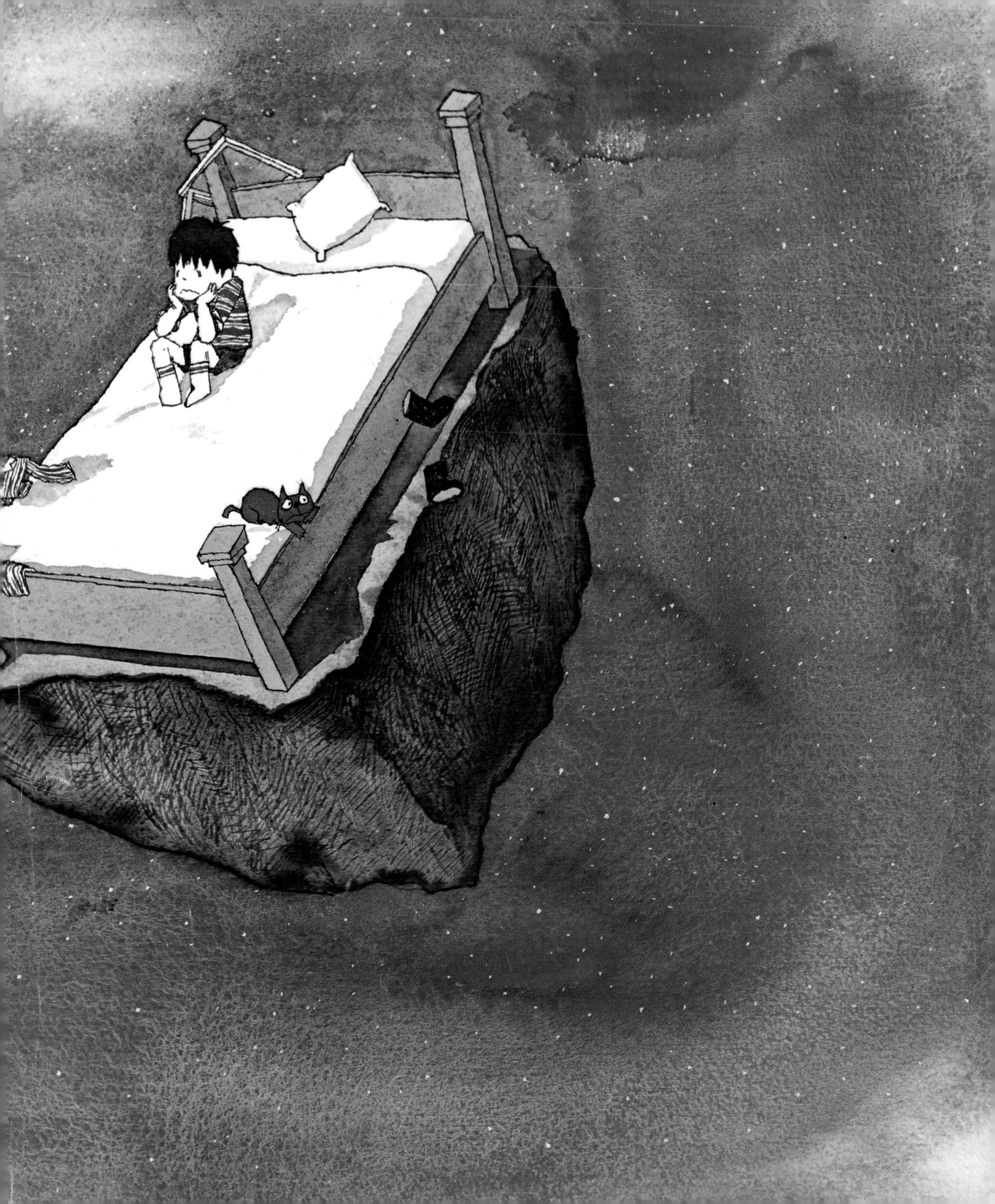

"Why was I so angry?" he thought.
He never did remember.
Can you?

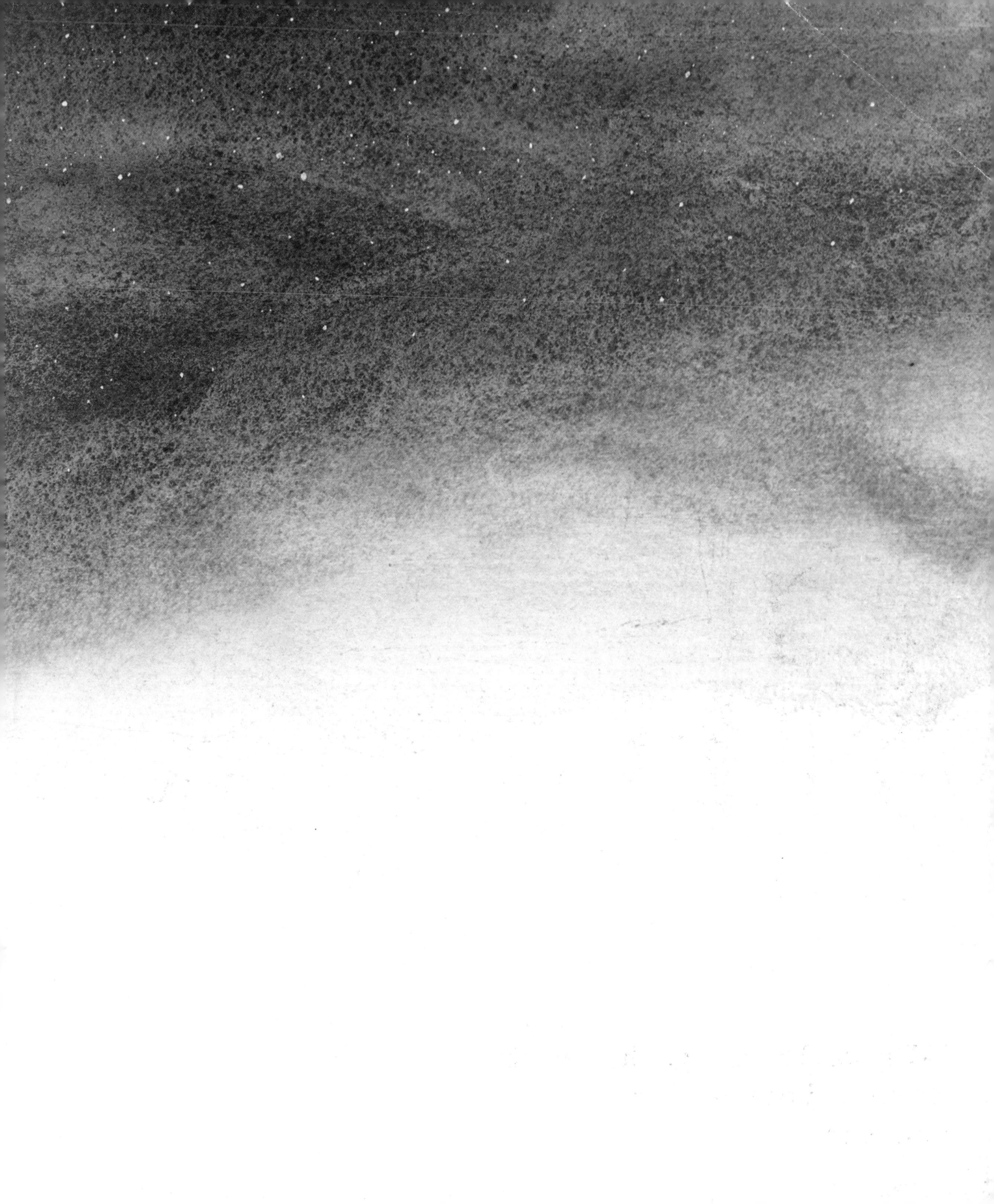

Other titles by

Satoshi Kitamura

A Boy Wants a Dinosaur (text by Hiawyn Oram)

Comic Adventures of Boots

From Acorn to Zoo: and Everything in Between

Igor, The Bird Who Couldn't Sing

In the Attic (text by Hiawyn Oram)

Me and My Cat?

Ned and the Joybaloo (text by Hiawyn Oram)

Once Upon an Ordinary School Day (text by Colin McNaughton)

Pablo the Artist

Sheep in Wolves' Clothing

UFO Diary

What's Inside?

What's Wrong With My Hair?

When Sheep Cannot Sleep